ENZO's
VERY SCARY HALLOWEEN

Garth Stein
Illustrated by R. W. Alley

HARPER
An Imprint of HarperCollinsPublishers

For Pepper,
the Amazing Tree-Climbing Dog
—G.S.

To Cassie, Max, Amy, and Chris—
trick-or-treaters of yore
—R.W.A. and Z.B.A.

"Tell us about Halloween, Daddy," Zoë says one fall evening. "But tell it the scary way!"

"What if Enzo gets frightened?" Denny asks.

I look up from my spot at the foot of Zoë's bed.

"Enzo," Zoë says to me sternly, "Halloween is about magic spells and monsters, but don't be afraid!"

Afraid? Why would I be afraid?

Denny turns out the light. He clicks on a flashlight and holds it below his chin so it shines a spooky light on his face.

"On Halloween," he whispers, "spirits and goblins run through the neighborhood. Witches fly on brooms, and dragons befriend fairy princesses! And the neighborhood will be haunted by ghosts forever if the people don't give treasures to all the creatures they see!"

"I can't wait!" Zoë shrieks. "It's *so* much fun, Enzo!"

Fun? It's going to take all my energy to protect us from this impending invasion. I hope I am up to the task.

Over the next week, Denny's prophecy begins to come true. Each day, more houses on our street become haunted: giant spiders weave webs on porches, gravestones appear on lawns, and pumpkins try to sneak into people's houses. They are evil

pumpkins, with sneering, demonic faces, but they're very slow moving, so we should be able to escape their evil spells. (I have never trusted a pumpkin.)

One evening Denny brings a pumpkin into
the house, and I am immediately suspicious.
"We're carving the jack-o'-lantern tonight!"
Zoë announces excitedly.

After dinner, Denny places the pumpkin on
newspapers he's laid out on the kitchen table. He rubs
his hands together like a mad scientist, and then he
picks up a kitchen knife!

I can't bear to watch; I lie down in the corner and
cover my eyes.

"It's alive!" I hear Zoë say.
I lift my head. The kitchen is
dark except for a flickering light.

I see Zoë with her magic wand, and
then I see the pumpkin, which has been
transformed into a demon.

Its eyes glow, and its grin
flickers with fire in its belly. I feel
my hackles rise and I growl softly,
my eyes fixed on the demon.

"I think Enzo is scared," Denny says.

Denny blows out the candle, and Zoë gives me a hug.

"Don't worry, Enzo," she says. "I'll protect you."

I relax a bit, but not entirely. I fear that Zoë's magic has accidentally released an evil pumpkin spirit inside our house.

The night of doom—Halloween—is soon upon us. I am very nervous. I go downstairs and I'm frightened to see that Zoë isn't Zoë anymore!

"Look, Enzo," Denny says. "Our little girl has been transformed into a fairy princess!"

I sniff in her direction. She still
smells like Zoë, but she looks different.
"It's your turn to transform, Daddy,"
she says, and she waves her wand.
"I'll be right back!" Denny says.

"And you, too," Zoë says to me.
What? I think. Me? No!

She pulls a bundle from a bag.
I try to escape, but she traps me.

She wraps a strange blanket
over me and snaps things
around my neck and haunches.

Then she taps me with her
magic wand. I bark, trying to
fend off the magic spell!

"I dub thee Enzo the Dragon!"
she says.

I don't feel transformed. I wonder
if my barking has countered the
effects of her spell.

Denny returns to the kitchen, but he isn't Denny at all! Zoë's magic wand has changed him into a scarecrow, with straw coming out of his sleeves and neck. His eyes peer out of a canvas sack with a face drawn on it, and he's wearing a dark hat.

"Isn't this fun, Enzo?" Zoë cries, laughing.

I want to think it's fun. I really do. But I don't feel the fun.

Before I can resist, the scarecrow snaps a leash on my collar and leads me to the front door. I catch a glimpse of myself in the mirror: the transformation has taken root. I have sprouted spikes on my back, and I have wings. I have become a dragon!

It's the jack-o'-lantern's fault! Surely Zoë never would have done this
to me. Denny and Zoë have fallen under the jack-o'-lantern's evil spell!
"Now we go trick-or-treating," Zoë tells me. "This is the good part."

The houses in the
neighborhood are glowing
with evil energy. A layer of fog
covers the lawn of one house,
and a mummy paces back and
forth looking for victims.

Another house has been transformed into a monster with fire in its eyes. Its mouth spews smoke as it awaits its dinner.

As we walk to Zoë's friend's house, I see that every child in the neighborhood has been transformed into a creature of some kind!

A goblin kneels down before me. "A real dragon," he says.
I bark and, to my surprise, the goblin falls over backward
and writhes on the floor.

"It breathes fire!" the goblin howls. "Run from the
fire-breathing dragon!"

I'm stunned. I didn't breathe fire. I barked! I bark
again to show him.

"Ahh!" the ghosts and goblins and witches shriek.
"Fire-breathing dragon!"

I try to tell them the truth—I am not a fire-breathing dragon—but each time I bark, the astronauts and ninja warriors and vampires shriek and run from me. I realize I *have* been transformed!

I don't want to hurt anyone by breathing fire, even if they are zombies and Frankenstein monsters and werewolves. I didn't ask to be transformed; it's an evil spell that is upon me! I am frightened by my *own* fearsome power!

I pull away from the scarecrow and take off running. If I cannot save myself from this evil spell, I must sacrifice myself so that others will survive!

I fly through the neighborhood, which is filled with terrifying things. I dodge this way and that, in and out, through hedges and around trees. When I look back, I see that all the creatures in the neighborhood are chasing me!

I veer down an alley. There are more monsters in front of me and more behind.

The monsters are everywhere!

I am cornered, but I refuse to unleash my terrible firebreath on these unfortunate creatures. They are about to pounce upon me, but I will not defend myself!

"Be still!" the fairy princess commands, stepping forward and halting the monsters with her magic wand.
"This is a friendly dragon who will do us no harm!"

"Don't be afraid, Enzo," Zoë whispers into my ear. "We know you're not a real dragon."

I'm not? I stop and look at her quizzically.

"Halloween is dress-up," she says. "We *pretend* to be monsters for a night. That's what makes Halloween fun. Being *almost* scared."

I am stunned by this revelation. I let out a small bark and am relieved when the princess is not burned to a crisp.

I peer up at the monsters and see: around the edges, they *do* look like kids in costumes! I stretch and do a downward-facing dog before Zoë.

"Be not afraid, little dragon," the fairy princess says, waving her wand high. "We need your help. Lead us to the houses so we may collect our treasures, and so this neighborhood will not be haunted forever!"

Proudly I lead the parade of pretend monsters to the houses and help them collect their treasures. The residents of each house fill the monsters' sacks with gold coins and jewels to appease them. And after each house, the monsters and goblins and vampires thank me for my guidance.

As our journey continues into the night,
the monsters slowly disburse, until finally
we are the only ones left in our parade.

The scarecrow picks up
the fairy princess and
carries her the rest of
the way home.

When we arrive, I am relieved to
see that our house is still there and
has not been haunted forever.

The scarecrow sets the fairy princess on her bed and takes off her shoes. She waves her wand one last time.

"The spell is broken," she says sleepily.

"All Hallow's Eve is over," the scarecrow agrees. He's no longer wearing his hat or his mask, so I know he's turned back into Denny.

I bark twice because I am happy to see him and Zoë again.

"That's right, Enzo," Denny says. "It's all over…until next year!"